SEASONS OF FUN: WINTER

by Finley Fraser

Consultant: Beth Gambro
Reading Specialist, Yorkville, Illinois

Minneapolis, Minnesota

Teaching Tips

Before Reading
- Look at the cover of the book. Discuss the picture and the title.
- Ask readers to brainstorm a list of what they already know about winter holidays. What can they expect to see in the book?
- Go on a picture walk, looking through the pictures to discuss vocabulary and make predictions about the text.

During Reading
- Read for purpose. Encourage readers to think about the special days in winter as they are reading.
- Ask readers to look for the details of the book. What is happening?
- If readers encounter an unknown word, ask them to look at the sounds in the word. Then, ask them to look at the rest of the page. Are there any clues to help them understand?

After Reading
- Encourage readers to pick a buddy and reread the book together.
- Ask readers to name three winter holidays from the book. Go back and find the pages that tell about these days.
- Ask readers to write or draw something they learned about winter holidays.

Credits:
Cover and Title page, © Shutterstock/Anatoliy Cherkas and © iStock/DaveAlan; 3, © Shutterstock/Hannamariah, © Shutterstock/jamakosy; 5, © iStock/manonallard; 7, © iStock/Patrick Chu; 8–9, © Shutterstock/Mordechai Meiri, © iStock/FamVeld; 10, © Alamy/Cultura Creative RF; 12, © Shutterstock/Iryna Kalamurza; 13, © Shutterstock/VCoscaron; 14, © iStock/AndreyKrav; 16–17, © Getty/Jeff Swensen; 18–19, © Shutterstock/1981 Rustic Studio kan; 20, © Shutterstock/Gizele; 21, © iStock/svetikd; 22, © Getty/Alex Wong, © Shutterstock/KLiK Photography, © Shutterstock/Marina Zezelina; 23, © iStock/Nadezhda1906, © iStock/AvailableLight, © Shutterstock/Egoreichenkov Evgenii, © Shutterstock/alexkich

Library of Congress Cataloging-in-Publication Data

Names: Fraser, Finley, 1972- author.
Title: Winter holidays / by Finley Fraser.
Description: Bearcub Books Edition. | Minneapolis, Minnesota : Bearport
  Publishing Company, [2021] | Series: Seasons of fun: Winter | Includes
  bibliographical references and index.
Identifiers: LCCN 2021009299 (print) | LCCN 2021009300 (ebook) | ISBN
  9781647478865 (Library Binding) | ISBN 9781647478919 (Paperback) | ISBN
  9781647478964 (eBook)
Subjects: LCSH: Winter--Juvenile literature. | Holidays--Juvenile
  literature. | Winter festivals--Juvenile literature.
Classification: LCC QB637.8 .F728 2021 (print) | LCC QB637.8 (ebook) |
  DDC 394.261--dc23
LC record available at https://lccn.loc.gov/2021009299
LC ebook record available at https://lccn.loc.gov/2021009300

Copyright © 2022 Bearport Publishing Company. All rights reserved. No part of this publication may be reproduced in whole or in part, stored in a retrieval system, or transmitted in any form or by any means, electronic, mechanical, photocopying, recording, or otherwise, without written permission from the publisher.

For more information, write to Bearport Publishing, 5357 Penn Avenue South, Minneapolis, MN 55419. Printed in the United States of America.

Contents

Holiday Fun 4

The Story of Groundhog Day 22

Glossary 23

Index 24

Read More 24

Learn More Online 24

About the Author 24

Holiday Fun

It is time for winter fun!

There are many fun days in the winter.

Some of them are holidays.

I love winter holidays!

Christmas is in December.

My family puts up a tree.

We put lights on the tree.

It looks so pretty!

My friend **celebrates** Hanukkah.

It lasts for eight nights.

People light **candles**.

They play a game with a spinning top!

Kwanzaa is another winter holiday.

It **honors** African American ways of life.

Families come together.

People light black, red, and green candles.

January 1 is New Year's Day.

It is the first day of the new year!

We have a party.

Happy New Year!

Martin Luther King Jr. Day is in January.

On this day, we remember Martin Luther King Jr.

He believed all people should be treated fairly.

February 2 is **Groundhog** Day.

Did the little animal see its **shadow**?

There will be six more weeks of winter!

Valentine's Day is all about love!

It is on February 14.

I give my friends cards shaped like hearts.

Winter holidays are fun.

I love them all!

Which winter holiday do you like best?

The Story of Groundhog Day

On February 2, 1887, the first Groundhog Day came to the United States from Germany.

People watched a groundhog. If the groundhog saw its shadow, that meant six more weeks of winter. If not, there would be an early spring!

Today, there is still a big party in Pennsylvania. The groundhog is named Phil.

Phil

Glossary

candles sticks made of wax with wicks that can be burned

celebrates does special things on a certain day

groundhog a small animal with brown fur and long front teeth

honors shows respect

shadow a dark shape made when something blocks light

Index

Christmas 6
Groundhog Day 16, 22
Hanukkah 8
Kwanzaa 11
Martin Luther King Jr. Day 15
New Year's Day 12
Valentine's Day 19

Read More

Grack, Rachel. *Valentine's Day (Blastoff! Readers: Celebrating Holidays).* Minneapolis: Bellwether Media, 2018.

Markovics, Pearl. *Hanukkah (Happy Holidays).* Minneapolis: Bearport Publishing, 2018.

Learn More Online

1. Go to **www.factsurfer.com**
2. Enter "**Winter Holidays**" into the search box.
3. Click on the cover of this book to see a list of websites.

About the Author

Finley Fraser is a writer living in Portland, Maine. He once went to the Groundhog Day celebration in Punxsutawney, Pennsylvania!